# SEVENTH GRADE BLUES

**Nathaniel Robert Winters**

**A novel for young adults or the young at heart**

THE BUFFALO PUBLISHING COMPANY

OF THE NAPA VALLEY

**"May you always keep your youth."**

**Mark Twain**

Chapter One

## The Runaway

Did you ever have a really bad day? You know, the kind where nothing goes right? So bad you want to run away? Well, last Wednesday was that kind a day for me.

Let me tell you; running away was not my best idea.

My name is Roger Raintree.

I live in Middletown, right in the middle of the good old U.S.A.

My favorite things are: baseball, good friends, pizza and now that I'm in the seventh grade, maybe even girls.

I go to Middletown Middle School in the middle of the suburbs of St. Louis, Missouri.

Wednesday morning, first thing when I got up, I had to go really bad, so I went. I was sitting there reading the sports scores when my older brother, 'Big Bird', yelled at me, "Roger, stop stinking up the bathroom. I need to get in there."

My brother's real name is Joseph or Joey. I'd tell you why everybody calls him 'Big Bird' but that's another story.

"Okay already. I'm just about done," I yelled back through the door. So I finished my business, opened the door and he punched me hard on the arm.

"That's for stinking up the whole place."

"Mom, Joey hit me hard," I yelled down to her in the kitchen.

"Joey, stop hitting your brother," she called back. Like that's going to stop him.

Dad would be more helpful here. He is good at keeping the Big Bird away from me but he left early to commute to work in the city.

I jumped into most of my clothes but I didn't have a clean shirt cause I forgot to give my mom my laundry. I picked out the one that looked the cleanest and pulled it on, but I forgot to give it the underarm smell test. That would become a big problem.

Mom had a cold so her voice sounded funny. "Grab a peanut butter and jelly sandwich, and drink your milk."

"Yuck, Mom, not chunky peanut butter, you know I hate chunky."

"Yes I know, but Joey likes chunky and it's his turn," she says.

From her voice I could tell her nose was stuffy and she wasn't feeling good but I couldn't help myself. Mockingly I said, "It's chunky Big Turds' turn, the stupid big butthead."

She gave me one of her killer looks and I stopped real fast. Mom is a high school teacher and she could say more with one look than most people could say with a whole speech.

I noticed in the mirror my hair was sticking up wildly. I tried the comb, then the brush but I couldn't get it right. Finally I gave up, shrugged my shoulders. I guess it's also going to be a bad hair day.

I was late for the bus so I sprinted fifty yards and hopped on just before it left. I was already sweaty so I picked an empty seat.

The bus pulled into the next stop. Then on that day, of all days, Sharon, just about the cutest girl in school, slid into the seat next to me.

She looked up, then crinkled her pretty nose and shouted, "Oh my God Roger, you smell so bad. It's like something died in your shirt." She grabbed her book bag and ran to another seat.

That's it, I thought. I'm totally messed up. I can never ever go to school again.

I zoomed to the front to get off the bus but evil driver, Miss Evans, the twin of Oz's Wicked Witch of the West, yelled,

"Sit down Roger!"

Ignoring her, I moved my body toward the door. My eyes had misted up but I can't cry in front of everyone. I felt it slowly moving down my face like a slug, the wet tear. Miss Evans repeated, "Roger you must sit down now!"

The next thing I knew I was pounding on the door. "Let me out, let me out, LET ME OUT!"

Wicked Witch pulled over and the door to freedom opened. I jumped out and heard, "Bus 5 to base, we have a problem."

I sprinted away, realizing I was in big trouble and headed straight home.

I felt safe at my house for the moment cause no one was home. I changed the nasty shirt, finally finding a clean one that I never wear cause it's got the stupid Chicago Cubs on it.

I grabbed all my money, $6.77, two granola bars and a water, tossed them into my pack and I was off.

To where? I didn't know.

I tried to calm down while moving up the street. After fifteen minutes the granola bars were gone and I found myself in front of the mall.

I went in, but on a weekday morning it was dull, empty, and lifeless. I entered a shop and saw some cool stuff but I had little money to spend.

In the Apple computer store, the security guard's eyes followed me like I was a common thief.

I realized I was getting hungry as I passed the empty food court with their overpriced crappy stuff, and walked out the exit.

Drifting north away from the mall, school and neighborhood, I wanted to be away from my usual turf. Why? I didn't know. It seemed like a good idea at the time.

I was hiking by the side of the highway along an empty sidewalk when I noticed the man out of the corner of my eye.

I remembered that he had left the mall right behind me. Then he wandered out of my sight. Reappearing, he was moving up on me fast and he gave me the creeps. You know how some people make you nervous just looking at them? Well this guy was one of those, times five.

He had a straggly beard, olive-green army fatigues, a plain black ball cap and those weird mirrored sunglasses where you can't see a person's eyes. I walked faster, but he still gained on me…oh my, I thought I saw a knife in his hand.

I was frightened, like totally scared. I thought maybe I should make a run for it when I saw the diner, like an oasis in the desert. Our family ate there often. I sprinted to the door and crashed through like I was coming around third and the catcher was blocking home plate. I could almost hear the umpire yell; Safe!

I relaxed as the smell of pizza, pasta, fried chicken, and cheeseburgers overwhelmed my senses and my mouth watered. I slid into an empty booth. The whole place looked deserted. I figured it must have been after breakfast and before lunch.

A pretty waitress with short dark hair was watching me as I counted my money; while I glanced longingly at the menu. She was young but old, like twenty-five, a real grown up woman. She walked over and I saw her name tag said Becky.

Her face smiled at me with warm brown eyes. "Can I get you something sweetie?"

I looked away from Becky to my money and said, "I'll just have a Coke."

She slid her order pad and pen in her vest pocket and said, "I'll be right back."

I tried to think. What could I do now? I had almost no money and that creep might still be out there. I couldn't go home cause I'm in so much trouble.

Becky brought my Coke and a big plate of French fries. "Don't worry, the fries are on me." Then she looked at me with knowing eyes and asked, "Are you having a bad day?"

I felt surprise and tried to put a smile on my face. "Thanks," came out of my mouth but I wanted to say more.

"Is it okay if I sit a second?" she asked.

I nodded.

As she sat, she asked,

What's your name?"

After I told her, she said again,

"Roger, are you having a bad day?"

"How did you know?" I asked.

"Well, we all have bad days."

"You have 'em?"

"Sure," she said

I could smell her perfume. It smelled real good, like pretty flowers. You know, the kind that dad would bring home for mom.

She asked me, "Did you run away?"

Surprised, I asked, "Are you one of them psycho-people?"

She gave me a funny look; then giggled. "You mean psychic. No, I'm just concerned. I ran away once, just about when I was your age; about thirteen, right?"

"Twelve-and- a-half. You really ran away?"

"Yes, I did."

"Are you a mom?"

"No, I'm working here part-time while I'm going to college. I'm still very single."

"Oh," I said. It was quiet for a minute. She didn't say anything, just waited for me. Finally I said "What did you do after you ran away?"

"When I came to my senses, I went home."

I sighed. "I can't go home. I'm in too much trouble. Mom and Dad are going to kill me."

"What in the world did you do that was so horrible?"

I told her all about what happened on the bus.

She smiled; then laughed. "Is that all? Okay, let me tell you two little secrets. First of all, that girl Sharon wouldn't have sat next to you if she didn't like you. Wear some clean clothes from now on. She'll come around."

"Second, when you have a bad day, don't run away. Tell your mom or dad. They will understand. They have bad days too."

I thought about what she said and realized she was probably right. "How did you get so smart?"

Her face lit up with a laugh. "I don't know, maybe it's from being in college. Tell you what; give me your mom's phone number. I'll call her for you. You know; to break the ice."

"Really?"

"Sure."

I tapped the number on my cell phone and gave it to her. She took it and walked behind the counter. I could see her talking for a while and then she came back and gave me the phone.

"Your dad's coming. Your mom said to bring you a cheeseburger. Is that okay?"

"Sure, thanks." I was still a little worried about The Creep who scared me before I came into the diner. I told Becky about him and she told her manager. The police took him to jail the next day, but that's another story.

About a half-hour later, I was just finishing the cheeseburger and licking my fingers when my dad came in. He sat down next to me and ruffled my hair. "So I hear you're having a bad day."

"Yeah; sorry Dad. I hope I didn't mess things up for you at work."

"No, it's fine son. Mom called me and I was happy to come get you. I just took a long lunch and can finish my work at home."

"You know, when you have a bad day, Mom and I feel bad for you."

"Really?"

"Yes, absolutely."

I thought about it; then broke into a grin.

"Dad, would you do something for me?" I gave him all the money I had.

"Will you give this to my waitress for a tip?" With a laugh, he rubbed my hair again.

"Don't worry, I took care of the bill and gave her a really big tip. I think you should take this money, go over and give it to her yourself."

So I scooted over and gave Becky the money. She bent down and kissed me on the cheek then gave me a big hug.

"Thanks," I said, "you're the best waitress ever."

She looked at me, then at my dad and said, "Why is it that all the good men are either too young or too old?" She giggled, brown eyes twinkling.

Dad grabbed my hand. We walked out of the restaurant together.

So I don't really recommend running away when you have a bad day.

It's funny, cause I saw Becky the very next day…but that's another story.

Chapter Two

## The Wall Fell Down

I hated my seventh grade English class. Old Mrs. Schultz ran our class like she was Joe Stalin. You're probably wondering who that Stalin guy was. He was the dictator of the Soviet Union at the beginning of the Cold War. If you disagreed with him, you were usually either found dead or sent to Siberia; the part of Russia where polar bears go to freeze.

Let me explain how she ran her class and you'll see why we were all bored out of our skulls. She would start by lecturing about something, like parts of speech or independent clauses; whatever they are.

When most of us were almost good and asleep, she would wake us up by passing out our workbooks.

We spent the rest of class working in total silence. I kept one eye on the clock, hoping it would move faster. Even when the bell would ring we had to wait in rows to turn in our workbooks and sit back down.

Finally, when we were all seated and quiet, 'Grandma Stalin,' would say, "Class dismissed," and we would fly out of the room.

Every class was the same thing. The torture continued day after day. At least old Mrs. Schultz had consistency working for her.

If you said anything, your name would be put on the board. A second infraction and you would be sent off to Siberia (the principal's office). Mr. Roper would then sentence you to another hour of prison (detention) with Mrs. Schulz.

She would spend the time grading worksheets with her red pen, placing big X's on the papers. I guessed we would be stuck with Grandma Stalin for the rest of the year.

So, when I returned to school the day after my run-away-to-the-diner adventure, I didn't expect anything different. As a matter of fact, I came back into Mrs. Schultz's class in a foul mood.

I was knocked out of dodge ball in PE class on the second throw. Before I could react, the ball bounced off Larry Peterson's arm and smashed me right in the face.

Blood spurted out of my nose like Niagara Falls. So I spent the rest of my favorite class in the nurse's office.

Since my original T-shirt was looking all bloody, the nurse made me take it off and put on a plain white T-shirt; **how humiliating**.

I came into Mrs. Schultz's class with my head down. But I noticed a din of chatter spinning through the room. I looked up and standing next to Mrs. Schultz was my waitress Becky from the diner. What in the world? I wondered.

Mrs. Schultz addressed the class. "Students, I have a surprise. We are going to have a student teacher, her name is Miss Garner, and she comes highly recommended from the university. I believe student teachers should jump in with both feet; so Miss Garner will be teaching your class for the rest of the year."

You could almost hear the wild cheering going on in our heads. Then, lickety-split, 'Grandma Stalin' left the classroom.

I remembered reading that the Berlin Wall came down just before the Soviet Union fell apart. In my mind I saw a great wall toppling over. (You might notice, I read a lot about history.)

Everybody started talking. They wanted to know who knew what. I looked up at Becky and was a little worried about whether she could handle the likes of us. Then she raised her hand, just like she was going to ask all of us a question. I'm not sure how the magic happened, but in just seconds the class calmed down and put their hands up. Without saying a word Becky; Miss Garner, had total control.

"Excuse me; I have to use the seating chart with your class today. I'll try to learn your names as fast as I can."

"Let's put those workbooks away for now. I see you have been going over parts of speech. I want everybody in class to participate. I will call on you. No pressure. If you don't know the answer, I will help you along."

"Ready?"

"Who can give me an example of a noun and use it in a sentence?"

Almost everybody had their hands up. Miss Garner looked at the seating chart and said, "Laura?"

Laura thought for a second; then said, "Miss Garner is our new teacher. The noun being, well—**you**." Everyone giggled, including Miss Garner.

"Good," she proclaimed. "Sam, give me another example of a noun in a sentence."

"Mrs. Schultz is the noun: Mrs. Schultz high-tailed it to the office."

Everybody laughed

Miss Garner said, "While I want you to have a good time in class, it is not okay to be disrespectful to a teacher or to any student. Is that clear? Raise your hand if you understand."

Everybody's hand shot up. "Thank you, okay, let's continue." She called on a bunch more students.

Finally she called on me. "Now," she said, "let's try one that's a little harder. Remember, no pressure. This is not a test. Nobody can make fun of anybody else. Roger, use a noun as the object in a sentence."

I had to think real hard. Then, I couldn't believe it, but I remembered something from the workbook.

"I met my new teacher at the diner. Teacher would be the object."

Miss Garner smiled. "Excellent. It appears that this class has a pretty good knowledge of the parts of speech. So Monday, we will start story time."

I looked up at the clock. The period had flown by.

Miss Garner said, "I want to thank you, class. Great job, everybody."

The bell rang and everybody else skipped out. I took my time packing my books. I wanted to be the last to leave. I turned to our new teacher and said, "Excuse me, Miss Garner; I never knew English class could be fun."

"I'm glad you enjoyed our first class but you need to see this."

She showed me the local newspaper. "It looks like the police have captured your Creep."

"Wow!" I said…but that's another story.

Chapter Three

## Big Bird

It's time to tell you the story about how my brother became Big Bird. It all started way back when I was four and my family went camping out west in Rocky Mountain National Park.

Now, I don't remember most of this part of the story but it's been told countless numbers of times at family get-togethers, holidays and even on a TV show.

One thing I do remember about that trip was walking down a wide forested trail with my mother. The world looked very green, greener than I had ever seen before. The air smelled like the pine cleaner my mom uses to clean the house before company comes.

A red fox came around the corner moving toward us in a jog, chased by a group of crows. They took turns picking him on his head and attacking other parts of his body. The fox barely looked at us as he tried to make his escape from the formation of black birds on aerial assault. I can still remember the look of sadness on the fox's face. It was like we were in a cartoon.

"Mom, why are those birds chasing that poor fox?"

"I don't know. Maybe he was trying to steal their eggs."

The whole image seemed terribly funny. I couldn't stop laughing but I felt bad for the fox.

So, let's get back to my brother's story. Our family tent was under an old oak tree. The camp was so quiet, especially in the mornings and evenings when everyone was wrapped in their sleeping bags. We could hear a bird singing a sweet song just above in the oak tree. The cool thing was that Joey started imitating the bird with a whistle. It sounded so much like the original, that the bird started singing to him.

Mom told us that the boy birds sing for a mate. If the girl bird likes his singing, she will return his call. My parents would look up the name of the bird later. It was called a blue-tip-yellow-belly-flycatcher; a big name for such a little bird.

Now this whole bird thing doesn't sound like such a big deal, does it? Yeah, well, don't tell my family that. Both my sets of grandparents thought Joey's bird trick was amazing.

Grandpa Lewis called it, **"The cat's meow."**

At any family gathering, Joey's bird trick would take center stage.

He even got to be on David Letterman's, 'Stupid Human Tricks' segment, on the late night television program.

There was this science class that went on the show every year and did bird imitations. So my grandparents wrote in and Joey got to join the class making bird calls on Letterman.

After that show, everybody started calling Joey, 'Little Bird.' Joey hated the nickname, but he had no choice. That's what everyone called him.

I think one of the reasons he didn't like the title of Little Bird was that he was quite short for his age. I was two years younger but we were the same height by the time he was in sixth grade.

Just down the street from us lived a guy named David Kearney. He was a year older than Joey, much bigger and was a true butthead bully.

Everybody tried to stay away from his house. He yelled nasty stuff, and if you were stupid enough to yell something back, he would come at you and start punching.

Once he held me down with his knees on my shoulders and spit in my face, while he laughed like a crazy man.

Between six and seventh grade, Joey shot up like corn in Kansas. By eighth grade he was powerful and almost six feet tall. Joey would always pick on me, but I knew he was just playing around. He never hit me with any power behind it; lucky me.

It was when he was in eighth grade that Joey happened to be walking by David Kearney's house, when the bully was picking on me again.

David had me cornered. My brother walked up and said, "Listen butthead." (He didn't really say butt or head, but I thought I better clean it up before I wrote it down). "If you ever mess with my brother again, I'll beat the snot out of you."

I could see David thinking about the situation for a second. But he wasn't about to give up his turf so easily. He spit out the words, "What are you going to do Little Bird, peck at me with your beak?"

Big mistake. Joey stepped in and punched him right in the eye. Down went Kearney, toppling like a tree cut down by a chainsaw. His face swelled up the size of a grapefruit below his eye. He started to get up but fell down again.

We took off. We didn't want to deal with Mr. Kearney. David's father was even nastier than his son. Maybe that's why David was so mean, having to live with that guy.

The police would come to the Kearney house just a few months later, but that's another story.

Anyway, the story of the punch spread like bumblebees in springtime. I would never have to worry about the bad bully up the street again.

David Kearney was out of school for a week. When he returned, his black eye was the evidence of Joey's powerful punch.

To the kids at school my brother had grown from, 'Little Bird,' to 'Big Bird.'

## Chapter Four
### The Creep

Let's get back to the story about that creepy guy who chased me into the diner after I ran away. Do you remember that Miss Garner showed me the newspaper article at the end of class? Here's the article:

### Body Found
### Homeless Man Arrested

A homeless man was arrested yesterday, after the West Middletown Police found the body of a man in Lincoln Park at 12:07 PM. The name of the deceased is being withheld pending notification of his family.

The homeless man, Dale Parker, has been charged with second degree murder. Mr. Parker has a long brown beard and was wearing green Army fatigues and a plain black baseball cap at the time of his arrest. If you have any information please call the West Middletown Police, at 555-1212

Feeling a bit uneasy, I asked Miss Garner, "That murdered person could have been me. What do you think I should do?"

"I think that you should talk to your parents about this. It's important that you get help with this situation. Then it will be up to your mom or dad to decide what to do."

I thought about it all evening and figured I would just lay low for the night. After all, the police had him in custody and I didn't see anything about a murder.

The next morning I read the front page of the paper, even before the ball scores or comics; a first for me.

The newspaper reported that the victim was Aaron Johnson, a security guard at the mall. The coroner placed the time of death about 10 AM. The article also said that Mr. Johnson was shot and the murder weapon had not been found.

10 AM, how could that be? We both left the mall just after ten and I went into the diner at about 10:45. He was still a half-hour from Lincoln Park, even if he walked quickly. The victim had been shot? Wow, I never saw the Creep with a gun. I thought he had a knife in his hand.

On the way to school, I told Big Bird. He said, "Let's go to the park after school and check it out." I thought about it for a second, and then said, "Okay, I'll meet you at home. We'll go faster by bikes."

Right after school we grabbed a snack and took off. Joey was on his bike and I was on our neighbor Sara's bike.

Even riding bikes, it took a half-hour to get to West Middletown's Lincoln Park.

That plastic yellow crime tape you see on TV surrounded two sections of the park.

We left our bikes and walked up to the closest one. "This is the crime scene," said my brother dramatically.

"I think I see dried blood on the grass over there," he said, looking with his binoculars, not wanting to disturb the police lines.

I searched the ground outside the tape. About thirty feet away I found a spent shell casing. Then I found another, of a different kind.

"Look at this," I said to Big Bird. "What do you think?"

"It could be that more than one person took a shot at the victim."

We walked over to the other taped area. I said to Joey, "The newspaper article said that this was Mr. Parker's campground."

I started searching around the area. I looked next to the tape and behind a bush. My mouth dropped open. There it was; the knife that had been in the Creep's hand before I escaped into the diner. Except it wasn't a knife at all. Now that I could see the whole thing, the metal object was just a fancy can opener.

Having watched many detective shows on TV, I used a gloved hand to pick up the object. That way I would not leave any fingerprints. I showed it to Big Bird and said, "This is what was in his hand. Maybe I was wrong about that guy. He wouldn't try to mug me with a can opener. He was probably just looking for a place to eat. Maybe the police are wrong too."

"Are we going to take that to the police?"

"No, we should take it home and show it to Dad. I remember something Miss Garner said: 'Talk to your parents'."

I carefully placed the can opener in my backpack and we hopped on our bikes. As we started to pedal away, I heard a car across the street burn rubber. The engine made a loud roar. I noticed the car was a rusted-out old Dodge; the kind they used to make with the big V-8 engines. I wondered if somebody had been watching us.

We got home, parked our bikes and I smelled Mom's cooking as we walked into the house. "Yum, meat loaf," I said, passing through the kitchen.

Mom looked at us and asked, "Where have you guys been?"

"Just out for a bike ride." I said innocently. I didn't want Mom to tweak out.

"Well go wash up you two; your dad will be home any minute. Dinner's ready."

During dinner, we explained to Dad where we were and what we found.

He said, "I don't think that was wise. That was a dangerous thing to do."

Mom gave us one of her evil schoolteacher looks that said, "You should know better."

Dad frowned. "You realize how serious this is, boys. It's a murder investigation."

Then he said, "I'm calling my friend Mel, the lawyer. I think we need to visit the West Middletown police and Mr. Parker."

At the station I was questioned by a police detective, flanked by my dad and his friend Mel Simmons. I handed the police officer all the evidence I had taken from the park. He told me that this evidence would not hold up in court.

Mr. Simmons smiled, showing total confidence. "I don't think this is going to have to go to court. I'd like to see Mr. Parker now."

"Parker has a public defender. He would have to give his permission," replied the policeman.

Mr. Simmons presented his legal argument that was beyond the officer's knowledge of the law. The policeman shrugged his shoulders in surrender. "I'll bring the prisoner to Visiting Room One."

Mr. Simmons, my father and I awaited Parker. I must say I was a bit nervous. The last time I saw this man he seemed to be dangerous.

But the man that the policeman brought into the visiting room looked nothing like The Creep.

His beard was gone. Now clean-shaven, his hair was short and neatly combed. His ratty, dirty clothing had been replaced with clean prison dungarees. Mr. Parker was actually a good-looking young man.

I told him about my encounter with him a few days earlier. He gave a sad laugh when he heard my description of him.

Then he started telling his story. It turns out that Dale Parker was a U.S. Army Special Forces veteran with three tours in Afghanistan. From all the combat and stressful stuff that he had gone through, he had something called PTSD, (that's what the Army calls someone who is suffering mentally from bad war stuff). When he came home from the war he had trouble relating to people and getting a job.

Deciding he needed a fresh start, he hit the road in his old Toyota. Parker found odd jobs here and there. Unfortunately, his condition left him uncomfortable in one place; so he kept moving.

Then his car broke down and he had to leave it by the side of the road. That made it even harder for him to find showers and clean clothes. He realized he was looking more and more messed up, like a homeless bum.

He hitched a ride and got dropped off in West Middletown and he set up camp at Lincoln Park. Hiding his stuff, he went off to try and find some work at the mall in Middletown. But when he went into the bathroom to get cleaned up, the security guard hassled him and demanded that he leave.

That was where I came into the picture.

We left the mall at the same time.


Mr. Simmons said, "This is such an obvious case of injustice, Mr. Parker, that I will take your case *pro bono*." (That's when a lawyer does it for free.)

"What about my public defender? He wanted me to cop a plea."

"We'll fix that; just sign here." Mr. Simmons pointed to a paper and Parker quickly signed.

"I'm your attorney now, Dale"

Mr. Simmons made some calls and fifteen minutes later Dale Parker was out on bail. The charges were dropped the next day.

Mr. Parker was definitely not a creep. I had never been so wrong about someone before in my whole life. This story taught me so many valuable things about life that it would take me way too long to tell you about it.

Oh yeah, one more thing. About six months later I got an e-mail from Dale Parker.

He was out in California. Got a job as a security guard at a ritzy mall in Beverly Hills. He even had a pretty girlfriend and sent me her picture. Not too bad for a creep.

You might be wondering who killed the mall security guard. Well, that's another story.

Chapter Five

## Haters

There's no two ways about it, I hate haters. It's kind of embarrassing to bring up, but Middletown is in Missouri which was a slave state. But you know, the Civil War has been over for more than 150 years. You would think everybody would have gotten the word by now.

If you went out to the country, especially in the southern part of the state, you'd see those rednecks driving around in old pickup trucks with Confederate flags all over their rear windows. They acted like the Union never won the war. People like Abe Lincoln, Jackie Robinson, Martin Luther King Jr. and Nelson Mandela never existed.

Sometimes I wish those idiots would join the twenty-first century.

You're probably wondering why I'm even bringing this stuff up.

It had to do with Sara Fisher and her family. Remember when my brother and I went looking in Lincoln Park for evidence? I was riding Sara's bike. She had mine cause my boys' bike was faster than hers and she'd borrowed it to enter a race to raise money for earthquake victims.

Our families are real close. My parents were friends of Anne and Chuck Fisher before we kids were even born.

Sara's a year older than me and we have grown up together. She is more like a cousin than my real cousins, and she is one of my best friends.

Anyway, she was an only child until the big earthquake in Haiti. Her mom Anne's a doctor and she went to help out on that island, where the people had so little and lost so much.

Anne fell in love with a little boy with a broken arm named Maurice, who lost his parents. She set his arm and he stole her heart. It took six months of red tape but then Maurice came home to the Fishers and Sara had a little brother.

It took us a little while to get used to Maurice, but now he's just one of the family. He has a funny accent and of course if you know anything about Haiti, you would know he is black.

He didn't quite fit in with the other black kids in the neighborhood or with anyone else at first. But he finally made friends with all kinds of kids in his third grade class.

Sara and I often met at school before classes and hung out together for a bit with a bunch of other friends.

As I arrived at school on a cold day in early December, I could tell something was wrong the moment I saw Sara's face.

"What's up?" I asked.

"You know that I'm in the Exchange-Student Club at school, Sara said. I found the club's Facebook page, addressed to me."

*You @#$*& &Jew, ^%$#* N*&^%R lover. We will get you! A greeting from your local KKK Boyz.*

I can't write what the post really said but it was nasty, full of bad things about her being Jewish and her brother being black.

"Sara, this is awful. I can see why you're upset. Do you think it is really from the KKK?"

"I think it's just from some racist kid trying to cause trouble. I cried about it last night but now I'm just good-and-angry enough to fight back. I'm not going to first period. I'm taking this to the principal right now. I've got a plan."

"Good, I'm coming with you."

"What for?"

"For support; I'm not going let you have to do this all by yourself."

Sara smiled at me and said, "Okay Roger, let's do this."

Let me tell you, when Sara gets her mind set about something, there's no stopping her. The girl is a real bulldog. She didn't win that charity bike race when she borrowed my bike, but she finished in the top ten out of five hundred starters and raised the most money for the charity.

We breezed into the office like eager beavers and Sara asked to see Mr. Roper. His secretary said, "He is busy this morning. Put your name on the list and he will call you in from class if he gets a chance."

Sara dug her heels in, "We'll just wait here."

Mrs. Karl looked flustered. "If you two don't want to get in trouble, you better go to class."

That special look gleamed in Sara's brown eyes. "Mrs. Karl, with all due respect, I'm not the one who will get into trouble, because after I call the paper and my parents call a lawyer, Mr. Roper will be sorry he didn't speak to me." (I told you she is a real bulldog.)

Mrs. Karl came back with Mr. Roper. He said, "Sara, I've already talked to your parents about that Facebook page and we will investigate the matter. I'll call you out of class later."

"I am not going to class. Not with the KKK after me. Unless something is done immediately, I don't feel like the classroom would be a safe place for me. I'll just stay here."

He looked at me. "Why are you here?"

I wanted to squirm away but I looked at Sara and got confidence. "I'm here to support her," I said, my voice squeaking.

He commanded, "Go to class now!"

I folded my arms, "I'm sorry sir but if Sara's not going, I won't go either."

I guess he realized he couldn't get rid of me unless he dealt with Sara first.

Sometimes support can come from an unexpected place. Remember old Mrs. Shultz, the one from my English class? Well, she had been promoted to vice-principal. She came over to Mr. Roper and said, "John, I was in school in Missouri during World War II. With my last name I was called a Nazi and even assaulted. Why don't we see what young Miss Fisher has in mind?"

"Okay, Sara, what do you want?"

"Call a special assembly this afternoon. Put out the word discrimination will not be tolerated. Let's put these bigots on the defensive."

Mr. Roper took a moment. "Sara, I think you're right. But I think this assembly needs more time for organization. I'll read something over the loudspeakers today to get the word out. Then you and Mrs. Schultz can get other volunteers to come after school and work on this. We can have the assembly on Friday just before vacation. We are going to need your help. Are you in?"

"Absolutely, Mr. Roper."

"Okay, Mrs. Karl, would you give these two students a pass back to class please." He turned and walked into his office.

Outside the office, Sara gave me a high five, "Yes, we did it!"

I just smiled. I didn't really do anything but I still felt really good about myself as I headed off to class. Sara organized a Pride committee and I helped.

By the way, I forgot to tell you my ethnic background. My dad's family has been around St. Louis since before there was a St. Louis, even before the American Revolution. They came with the French explorers of the Mississippi. His side of the family tree has some interesting branches. My great-great-great-grandfather was a Sioux warrior and legend tells he fought at the Battle of Little Big Horn (on the Indian side). He met his white wife, a school-teacher, on a reservation in Oklahoma. They slipped into St. Louis where the local bigots were much more concerned about free slaves than Indians. My mom is from New Jersey; part Italian, Irish and Polish; she thinks. So, I guess I'm your typical American mutt. Cool, huh?

It was amazing what we accomplished in just one week. Sara got the media involved and a reporter came out to interview her. She was on the news.

The major objective was to have students sign a pledge, simple and to the point: "**I have pride in my cultural background and show respect for all others**."

Friday's rally was fantastic. Classes went half the day and the assembly was in the afternoon. There were bands – marching, rock and roll, rap and country; something for everyone.

The St. Louis sports teams lent a hand, sending players from the Blues, the Rams and the Cardinals to sign autographs. Ninety-seven percent of the students signed the petition. The other three percent lay low, not wanting to say anything.

Sara never received any more racist stuff. But there was a small group that still faced discrimination. That would come to a head soon. But that's another story.

## Chapter Six

### Where are the Oranges?

During Christmas vacation our family and the Fishers went to LA. The first few days, we stayed in Orange County. Then we went to Hollywood which was another story.

Disneyland was the first thing on our list. All of us except Maurice had been there before. Joey, Sara and I all complained; thinking we were too old for Mickey Mouse and Disney. What we didn't realize was how much fun it could be to watch as our 'little brother' see the place for the first time.

Growing up in Haiti, he didn't even have a TV. To him, Disneyland was like being on another planet. We caught his excitement like it was a disease, a really good disease.

The little guy laughed and giggled in happiness when Goofy and Pluto came up to him. I had forgotten how much fun the rides could be. Even the old Pirates of the Caribbean was fun because it was all so new to him.

The Haunted Mansion scared him out of his wits. He almost cried, but Sara put her arm around him and said, "It's not real, Maurice, just make-believe. I'll make sure nothing hurts you."

He looked at her just as a ghost jumped out in front of him. His eyes got big with fright for just a second. Then all of a sudden, he got it. He laughed, "Yes, I see; make-believe." He waved both arms at everything.

I figured that because Maurice had grown up without watching television or movies he never had the same chance to figure out that not all the stuff you see is real. It was only when Sara told him it was all make-believe that he could figure it all out.

Not everything you see is real life. I remembered that poor Maurice lived through an earthquake that killed his parents. No wonder the Haunted Mansion scared the heck out of him.

That day, it seemed like we tried to go on every ride. We stayed well into the night and watched the fireworks and the parade. Boy, we sure had a good time.

The next day we went to Newport Beach. I wanted to go into the water and learn to surf. But after I stuck my foot in that cold ocean water, I changed my mind. The Pacific Ocean at Christmas time in Southern California was really cold. I could see why all the local surfers were wearing wetsuits.

But our parents got two of these little plastic things for us. I'm not sure what they're called, but you could run up and jump on and skip along in the shallow water after the waves would glide in. We all took turns with the two 'wave runners,' or whatever they're called.

One time as I jumped on the board, my brother came up and knocked me off. It sent me splashing into the water. I was pissed off but I laughed.

You know how something can be good and bad at the same time. So I tried to knock him down. I hit him full blast and wound up on my butt. Sometimes it's not easy being the younger brother.

Don't tell that to Maurice, though. Sara doted on her little brother. She tried to get him to play with the board in the shallow water. He said with his broad smile, "No, no, no, that water is way too cold. When I swam at home the water was warm."

His eyes looked out at the ocean and I think he could almost see himself back in Haiti, swimming in the Caribbean with his first parents. I often wondered how much he missed them. He always seemed like such a happy kid.

That night our parents went out to dinner. It was Christmas Eve. We were left at the hotel, babysitting for Maurice. I certainly didn't mind, I was tired and sunburned from the beach. Besides, we got to order takeout pizza delivered to our room and could watch a movie on the hotel's big flat-screen TV. Maurice wanted to see *Toy Story*. I thought, no, not more Disney stuff again, really?

But when we started watching, I got totally into it. I forgot how good that movie was. The last time I watched, I was Maurice's age, laughing with my parents. Maybe you never get too old for Mickey Mouse stuff.

Christmas morning in Orange County didn't look or feel like Christmas. It appeared to be just another day of blazing blue skies and sunshine. In our two big adjoining rooms, we had a two-foot pathetic 'Charlie Brown,' Christmas Tree, complete with foil strips that kinda sparkled in the sunlight. We sang one Christmas song, something about a reindeer dancing with a dolphin and sleds with surfboards – something like that.

My dad, complete with a stick-on white beard, played Santa.

Our parents (or Santa) must have gotten a deal at the local mall because we each got a laptop computer. I was totally jazzed (yeah, we still say that in St. Louis). It was just what I wanted.

Maurice was really happy about getting a laptop instead of his usual toys. I wasn't surprised. The kid was an amazing student. I thought that Joey, Sara and me were good students but Maurice left us all behind. In third grade, he was already googling: The French Revolution, Napoleon and Haiti.

I asked him why he was such a serious student. He said, "Don't you know that in Haiti, I wouldn't have had this kind of chance, this kind of education?" Sometimes it takes someone from somewhere else to make us see how lucky we are.

As we drove away north on **The 5**, as the Southern Cal home dudes say, I realized I haven't seen one darn orange tree.

Chapter Seven
## A  Night to Remember

One of Sara's mom's best friends lived in Hollywood, actually in Beverly Hills.

Sandy Mills and Dr. Anne Fisher were co-captains many years ago, on the Liberty High School cheerleader team in Patterson, New Jersey.

I tried to think of Dr. Fisher as a cheerleader but it seemed strange. I guess it's hard to think of your parents or their friends as kids in high school.

Anyway, Anne's friend Sandy went to the University of Southern California for about a year, where she met Douglas Michael, yup, that Douglas Michael, the famous actor and the son of John Douglas Michael, the even more famous actor. The college romance led to marriage and a daughter, Shelly. In true Hollywood style, it also led to divorce.

Mrs. Mills invited all of us to stay at her house. Sara and Shelly were friends and kept in touch despite living so far away. They were about the same age and were together every few years when the moms would visit, usually in California. They would also e-mail and Skype. I remembered hearing about Dr. Fisher's movie star friend over the years but I didn't pay much attention. It just seemed like gossip that didn't concern me until I found myself at the front door of one of the fanciest houses I'd ever seen. The view looking down on LA wasn't bad either.

I overheard Dad whispering to Mom, "Our host must have had a pretty good divorce lawyer."

Sandy greeted us at the door with a big smile. When she saw Anne she gathered her in a big bear hug.

"Come in, come in, let me show you where you'll be camping out. Sorry Shelly isn't here to greet you. You know, it's Christmas and it was her dad's turn. She'll be here soon."

We worked our way up one of those grand curving staircases you see in the movies. I'm not sure how many rooms were in the upstairs but my parents were shown into one bedroom and Joey and I were delivered to another.

I did notice that the silver ashtray in the room was polished like fine jewelry. I was afraid to touch anything.

"We've planned lunch around the pool, if that's all right, and then we'll all head down to Venice Beach," said Mrs. Mills.

There was no doubt about it, Mrs. Mills was very pretty. I don't usually notice that much about how other kids' parents look but she was movie-star good-looking. She was in a few movies before she was married but I haven't seen any. As we changed into our swimsuits, Big Bird filled me in on the latest magazine gossip about Sandy Mills.

The pool was on the back uphill side of the house, next to the tennis courts. Wild plants and trees grew beyond the fence. As I plunked down on a lounge chair with the golden sun gleaming down, I thought; this is nice, I could get used to this.

Drinks were served by a woman with a Spanish accent. Sandy introduced us to Carlotta, who helped out with the chores but also lived with the family and was a college student. Carlotta smiled at us and gave a quick wave, then disappeared back into the house. She came back out with a tray full of sandwiches.

I was about halfway through my ham-and-cheese when I stopped in mid-bite. The most beautiful girl I had ever seen just walked out to the pool. The moment I saw her I knew something inside me changed. She wore the world's smallest, reddest bikini and even though I knew she was the same age as Sara, she was more...er…her body was more mature. I couldn't take my eyes off her. The girl glowed in the sun like some kind of a Greek goddess that we learned about in history class.

We all got up to greet her and she gave Sara's family hugs. When she put out her hand to shake mine, I hoped she wouldn't notice the perspiration on my palm. But when we started talking she sounded just like any other kid, so I relaxed.

We all jumped in the pool and started playing Marco Polo. After I got to know her better, things were cool.

When we got to Venice Beach, the plan was to meet back at the cars later for dinner. We older kids went one way and our parents took Maurice and went off in another direction. Shelly played tour guide.

Venice Beach was incredible. It wasn't as pretty as Newport, but it was a lot bigger and had so much going on.

A number of the kids looked like hippies from the 60's. There were lots of kids from all ethnic groups that looked like they might be gangbangers, you know the guys with tattoos and long baggy shorts down almost to their ankles. And then of course there were all the pretty girls in bikinis or short shorts. Oh yeah, I could get used to this.

We put our blankets on the beach and then headed up the boardwalk toward Santa Monica. To the left was endless beach. To the right was the city of Venice.

On the boardwalk people were selling all kinds of stuff; art, T-shirts, bathing suits, even massages and tattoos.

It wasn't a real boardwalk made of wood, but a cement trail, almost like a little road without the cars. Girls and guys passed by on roller blades and bikes.

We strolled along and came upon a whole group of muscle-men lifting weights. When I say muscle-men, they were all built like the former Governor of California, a bunch of young Arnold Schwarzeneggers.

Just beyond these guys were people playing paddle tennis. It looked like fun.

The boardwalk thinned out to the north of the city and there were a ton of beach houses. There were people lying in the sun or out partying with loud music blasting. What a place!

We turned around and headed back to our stuff. And we spent the rest of the day just fooling around in the water and having a great time.


The last day, before New Year's Eve, we did one thing that was really interesting but also very sad. We went to the Holocaust Museum.

If you don't know about it you should. It represents the history of the atrocities the Nazis committed in World War II.

It's amazing how cruel people could be. But that's another story and it's not mine.

So go, if you get a chance. The trip to the museum made me even more proud of Sara and the stuff we did at Pride Day.


The time seemed to fly by. It was New Year's Eve and we had to leave the next day.

That evening Shelly and her mom threw a big party. The grown-ups were inside and the kids were out by the pool. Some people came all dressed up and some were casual; no rules.

I went with casual. Shelly descended the staircase in a blood-red mini-dress looking like, like what? How can I compare the most beautiful thing I had ever seen to anything else? The only thing that came close to what I felt seeing her was when the Cardinals won the World Series.

At the party, of course, we didn't know any of Shelly's friends but some were friendly and talked to us. I did notice that my brother, who always seemed comfortable around girls, seemed a little nervous around Shelly, kind of flirting awkwardly. I felt shy around her that night and never said much.

Before we knew it, we were counting down to midnight. There was a big-screen TV on the balcony next to the pool. Most of the crowd was a little young for the boyfriend and girlfriend thing. A few of the kids paired off to get ready for the midnight kiss.

Even in LA, which is three hours behind the East Coast, near midnight, the TV station was tuned into a recording of New York and the famous 'Ball,' dropping in Times Square.

With less than a minute left, I saw Shelly approach us. I was with Big Bird and Sara so I figured Shelly was coming to be with her guests for the big moment of celebration.

As the clock struck zero, Shelly put her arms around me, drew me in and kissed me right on the lips, a long dreamy kiss.

I really didn't know what to do or what I was doing. I figured I was supposed to close my eyes but I continued to stare into her California sky blue eyes. I watched her, she watched me. It didn't last more than seconds, but forever.

I stood there with my mouth as open as a summer barn door.

"Why…what…"

Shelly smiled a sly wicked smirk; then winked. "Sara told me you've never been kissed. I just wanted to give you something special. Nobody forgets their first kiss. It's nice to know you'll never forget me or this night. Happy New Year, Roger Raintree."

I watched as she turned and walked away, hips swaying. My fingers touched my numbed mouth and slowly my lips took the shape of a smile. Then I laughed. She's right, I'll never forget that night.

## Chapter Eight
### More Haters

I've known Marshall LaBeche since kindergarten. He was one of the guys who I spent hours playing ball with after school and during the summer. Marshall was always good at whatever he wanted do.

In the fifth grade, we did a class play. Of course, being in St. Louis, right on the Mississippi, we had to do *Huckleberry Finn*. I had a small bit part, but Marshall played Huckleberry and did a great job.

On the basketball court, he was a wizard. You know, the kind of player who can dribble through everybody, stop on a dime and hit a jump shot, or drive past the big guy and curl the ball around him into the basket.

Sara and I were sitting at the coffee house across from school. Sara said, "You should've seen the look on your face when Shelly kissed you. Too bad I don't have a picture. It was priceless."

We were both giggling about New Year's Eve when Marshall walked up. "Hey Roger," Marshall said, "How you doin'? Are you guys busy?"

"It's okay, Marshall. What's up?" I said.

I knew him much better than Sara. He looked uncomfortable.

"You know that thing that you did – the Pride thing? It was really important to me. It made me realize that I should be proud of who I am," Marshall said.

"I'm…coming out. I'm gay. Oh my God, that's the first time I've said it out loud!"

"No freaking way!" I said without thinking.

Sara immediately realized why Marshall was here talking to us. "Oh my goodness, Marshall. I'm so sorry, I left the gay people out of the Pride thing. It was a mistake."

Her eyes took that focus. I almost heard the bulldog in her growl. I knew action was about to follow.

Marshall said "Sara, this isn't your fight. It's my turn now."

I still was in shock. "Marshall, you're really gay?"

He laughed. "Did you think – because I can kick your butt at basketball – that I can't be gay?"

"No. Sorry. I didn't mean it that way, I just never guessed. How…how long have you known?"

He threw it right back at me. "How long have you known you were straight?"

I thought about it for a second. "I guess I've always been straight."

Marshall said, "I guess I always knew I was gay, even if I didn't want to be. It's not like I've ever had sex or anything, yet. I've never even been kissed by another boy."

My mind went in too many directions. I didn't know what to think except that I was on Marshall's side.

Sara took charge. "Meet me in front of the principal's office first thing tomorrow."

"I'm coming too," I said. "You know, for moral support."

So, as I walked home that evening, I thought about General Eisenhower and D-Day. General Eisenhower said to always choose your battles carefully. And then plan, plan, plan; and when you think you're ready, plan some more.

I know this cause I somehow always loved history. It was my favorite subject, besides PE, of course, especially stuff about World War II.

Sara was no Eisenhower. She was more like a rookie Marine lieutenant; no advanced planning for that girl, just attack – follow me! We're taking the hill!

It all worried me.

The three of us marched into Mr. Ropers' office. Sara, naturally, took charge and demanded to see the principal.

I had a strange feeling. Something felt wrong this time.

Mr. Roper flew out of his office. Immediately, anger showed on his face. "Sara," he said, "I've put up with enough of your nonsense. I'm not going to let you take over my school. Leave right now, or face suspension."

"Mr. Roper, this isn't right," Sara said. "I'm just trying to help out a friend. Gays shouldn't have been left out of Pride Day."

"I'm not going to argue with you, young lady. You have five seconds to leave my office."

Sara stood her ground. Yup, she was a Marine. No retreat possible.

Roper counterattacked. "Make out three suspension slips, Mrs. Karl, and call their parents. "You're all suspended for two days."

As we walked out of school, Sara announced, "If he thinks this is over -- **this ain't over!**"

That night, she gave me a list of calls to make. We were rounding up the troops. That next day at school we staged a demonstration.

Halfway into the third period, a majority of students walked out of class. The rest of that school day most of the kids marched around the school and carried signs of freedom.

What we didn't realize was that gay people didn't have the same sort of support that the ethnic groups did.

Within the next few days, I learned a lot about politics. Most of the kids at school supported the fight for gay rights.

But parents highjacked the debate. A strange alliance of rednecks and conservative church groups united against gay rights.

TV stations showed our demonstration. The Middletown Middle School debate was all over the Saint Louis local news. Reporters interviewed people from both sides including Sara and Marshall. They even made fun of the whole thing on **The Daily Show**.

Middletown's Mayor got into the picture. I guess he realized he would lose votes if he picked either side. So he tried to be the peacemaker and pull apart the big dogs going for each other's throats.

Two days later, Marshall, Sara and I met back at the coffee house. Marshall said, "This has gotten way out of hand. You wouldn't believe my Facebook page. It's blown up. Last night, a bunch of crackers came by and threw bags of dog crap on my lawn, yelling stuff like 'Get outta town, f@#$#t. @%&*&&%%$.'" (I won't list all the cuss words he told me.)

"I'm so sorry," Sara said.

I think she was a little shell-shocked.

"Maybe we can take a new approach," I said. "After all, most of the kids are still on our side."

"No," said Marshall. "I'm tired of people getting in the crossfire of my fight. My dad was offered a job in Palo Alto, that's in California. He took it. We're moving. He thinks people won't be so hostile toward gays in that part of the country."

"I really want to thank you. You two have been great friends. I'll never forget it."

We cried. We hugged. He started to walk away, then stopped on a dime, like he did playing basketball. Marshall did an about-face and saluted us like we were officers in his personal army.

In unison, we saluted back.

It all hit me hard, harder than my brother's punch to that bully David Kearney. I discovered that just because you believe you are on the side of something – something important – you don't always win. Important stuff, like freedom and justice, don't come easy.

I thought of Kunta Kinte, the slave; Nathan Hale, the Revolutionary patriot and Anne Frank, the Jewish girl who didn't live to see freedom.

Others, who struggled for years, like the soldiers in World War II fought so we can be free. I realized the people in the history books are as real as Marshall, Sara and me.

It was a little scary.

Chapter Nine
**Springtime Math: 6-4-3=2**

Middletown is a suburb of St. Louis. The mighty Mississippi flows right through the city. It was called the Gateway to the West during the frontier days.

If you ask anyone about the most popular people that came from St. Louis, they would probably come up with two names: Mark Twain and Stan "The Man" Musial. Mark Twain is legendary. I've heard him described as America's greatest author. He is definitely one of my heroes.

And let me tell you, everybody loved Stan Musial. He was the greatest baseball player ever to play for the St. Louis Cardinals. Greater than great; he was "The Man." Musial was a World War II hero, a quiet leader, a gentleman, Mr. Saint Louis.

I love baseball. You probably knew that when I told you I used to read the sports scores when I went to the bathroom. I know that football and basketball are more popular in many places but probably not in St. Louis. We love our baseball team.

Some of the most fun times I can remember were when Dad and sometimes Mom took us to the see the Cardinals play.

The Big Leaguers were always amazing. They made the hard stuff look easy; like turning a double play. If someone hit the ball to the shortstop with a man on first, the ball would swing around the infield faster than you could say, "Jackie Robinson." Man, all my years playing Little League, I never turned a double play.

I play ball all the time but I'm not that good. I'm not bad, just about average for a kid my age. It's funny, I'm not that good at math but I could tell you the batting average of each player, the ERA of every Cardinal pitcher and I could figure it to the decimal point.

Anyway, no more Little Leagues for me. I went out for the Middletown Middle School Marauders baseball team. I bet you can't say that name three times fast.

I felt lucky when I made the team as a substitute infielder. We had a pretty good roster and made it into the playoffs. Our best player was a stud by the name of Randy

Johnson. No not that Randy Johnson; the one who will be in the Hall of Fame. But the Randy Johnson who lived two blocks away. He was our best pitcher and hitter.

So, as I was saying, we were in the playoffs against West Middletown and Randy was pitching a killer game. He only gave up one hit and two walks the whole game. We were up one-to-nothing in the top of the last inning and loaded the bases with one out. The coach signaled for me to pinch hit for Ralph Jeffries, our starting second baseman. I figured it was because he struck out a lot and at least I usually made contact with the ball.

The first pitch I took, because it seemed inside, but the ump called, "Strike one."

I stepped out of the box, then back in, waving my bat as I looked for a pitch outside that I could drive to right field.

I swung hard and made pretty good contact but the hard grounder went right to the second baseman, who flipped it to the shortstop covering second, who fired a strike to first. The ball beat me by a darned step for a very amazing double play.

I couldn't believe it. We got nothing. I hung my head and sauntered back to the dugout when I heard Coach yell, "Roger Raintree, get your head out of your butt, you hit the ball hard. Get your glove and play second base."

I hop-stepped into the dugout, grabbed my mitt and jogged to position. The first baseman tossed me a few practice grounders and the umpire yelled, "Play ball, boys."

Johnson stood on the mound where he had been dominating a very good West Middletown team. He struck the first guy out on three pitches. Then the trouble started. Johnson got two strikes on the next West Middletown player but the little guy fouled off five good pitches before Johnson walked him. Then Randy walked the next two batters, just missing on some close ones. The bases were loaded with just one out. Coach knew our main guy was tired and in trouble as he strolled slowly toward the mound. Jeff Mason was warmed up and ready on the sidelines.

The whole infield gathered on the mound with Coach. "What do you think Randy?"

"I can reach back and bring it for a few more pitches. I struck this guy out last time."

"Okay, you deserve to give it a try. But if you don't get ahead of this guy, I will bring in Jeff."

"Understood, Coach."

We all returned to our positions and Coach to the top step of the dugout.

Johnson did reach back and blew a fastball by the batter. On the next pitch I looked in and saw the catcher signal for a curve. I thought Randy had thrown maybe five curve balls all game but he nodded his head, wound up and delivered a breaker, knee-high to the batter. The hitter was badly fooled and topped a roller to short.

Josh Randolph was our second best player and he attacked the grounder moving in and fired a pea to me covering second. I pivoted and the man on first slid towards my legs to take me out. Somehow I jumped and got just enough on my throw to…to what? It was really close. The Umpire delayed and looked carefully at the play. Finally the man pumped his fist. "You're out; ballgame."

I was on the ground, spilled by the runner. I realized we just turned a major league-style 6-4-3, a two-out double-play to win our first playoff game. We mobbed each other, celebrating on the mound.

Then it all continued as our families joined the team at the local pizza joint.

I forget that most people don't know how a baseball scorebook works. I've been around the game so much, baseball phrases seem second-nature. So, 6-4-3=2 is how you write a shortstop, to second base, to first base double play; for two outs in a scorebook.

The next game without Randy on the mound, we got swamped, but we all felt pretty darn good about the season.

Dad bought me a special present, an autographed Stan Musial baseball. How could ya' not just love the game!

## Chapter Ten
### Hate, Crime and Punishment

On an early March spring-like day, flowers bloomed and birds sang in hopes to attract a mate. Walking home in the neighborhood after school I heard my stomach growl. I knew it was almost snack time.

Suddenly, behind me, I heard the roar of a big engine. Glancing back I saw what seemed like a ghost or a nightmare. That rusted-out old silver Dodge stalked me like a lion after a zebra.

What is it doing here in my neighborhood? Before fright overwhelmed me, I took off towards my friend's familiar backyard. I hid behind the fence and waited until the sound of the big engine was gone.

Was it just my imagination? No, I recognized that car. The one I saw at Lincoln Park the day my brother and I looked for evidence there.

Carefully, I continued my journey home. Turning the corner to my block, I ducked behind some bushes…the car was parked next to my house.

Why was it there? Had the occupants seen Joey and me in the Park? Were they the killers? Questions danced through my head with terrifying results. I thought of dialing 911 but what would I say? There's a car sitting outside my house. (Yeah, the major crimes unit would come running with a story like that.)

Curiosity and hunger got the best of me. I left the bushes and tried to look confident as I walked past the car to my house. The man sitting in the passenger seat yelled, "Hey kid, come here."

I was going to run again. Then I saw the gun pointed at me. I froze, like a deer in the headlights. (I know this phrase is overused but it fits so well.)

Lights flashing, an unmarked police car pulled up behind the silver Dodge. Two plainclothes policemen got out of the flashing car. I recognized Joe Thornton, the detective that interviewed me.

The detective and his partner slowly approached the Dodge, guns drawn. "Get out of the car. Keep your hands where I can see them."

The Dodge peeled away. They didn't get far, as two other police cars blocked their way. For a moment the Dodge gunned its engine. But suddenly the evil car coughed and fell silent. The bad guys came out with their hands up. "Okay, okay, don't shoot!"

A policeman yelled, "Get down on the ground."

The bad guys dropped to the pavement. Two uniforms handcuffed the men on the ground and read them their rights.

I was waiting for a director to yell "Cut". This had to be a movie set. Right?—It just had to be.

Then Detective Thornton walked up to me and said, "Roger, are you okay?"

I swallowed for the first time since I saw the man with the gun. My body was still shaking.

"I guess I'm okay," my voice squeaked.

"You were never really in danger," said Detective Thornton. "We've tailed these guys since you described the silver Dodge to me. We caught them doing some bad stuff – I can't tell you the details – but your description led to this bust."

That evening I saw patrol cars in front of David Kearney's house. I caught a glimpse of David and his father being led away in handcuffs.

This is amazing, I thought, nothing like this ever happens in Middletown, for gosh sakes.

About eight o'clock that night, the doorbell rang. I ran to answer it. A uniformed police officer was standing by the door. He knew me by name. "Roger, I would like to talk to your parents."

"Dad, Mom; it's the police. They want you."

My father and mother shuttled the police officer into the back room and shut the door. Joey and I tried to listen in but could hear only mumbles. I whispered, "What you think they're saying?"

He whispered back, "I don't know, maybe something about the park."

The door opened. The police officer, shaking my father's hand said, "Thank your sons for us and thanks for all your help."

"What was that all about?" I asked.

Dad looked at me and Big Bird and said, "It appears that you two might have to testify at a trial. You guys found some really important evidence at Lincoln Park. It led to several arrests. They couldn't tell us much, but it seems like they made a really large drug bust."

"Holy crap!" Big Bird and I said, almost at the exact same time.

The next day, I was back to reading the front page before the sports and comics. Information about the bust spread around the school like a disease, a bad disease.

I learned that the two guys from the Dodge were charged with multiple counts of murder.

Mr. Kearney was allegedly involved and arrested and David was immediately sent to a youth home, pending an investigation.

It appears that white prison gangs, the KKK and other White Power maniacs were involved in major methamphetamine trafficking.

Within weeks, the cases were sewn up, with most of the bad guys taking plea bargains.

The police told us that we probably wouldn't have to testify.


In small-town Middletown, everybody finds out about everything. It's hard to keep secrets when people know people who know people.

It turned out that David's family's computers were confiscated during the drug bust. David's sixth grade sister Lisa was the one who sent the racist e-mails to Sara.

When she came back after suspension for sending the e-mails, Lisa Kearney was treated like a drunk Red Sox fan at Yankee Stadium. Nobody would go near her.

Lisa seemed like a pretty normal girl before the bust and her suspension over the e-mails. After that, she looked awful. There were deep bags under her eyes and she wore only black. Her hair dyed black, fingernails painted black and a bleak dark look in her eyes.

At lunch she was alone, totally alone, sitting by herself, looking rejected and sad.

"Sara," I said, "I feel so bad for her. You know she was probably abused by her father and brother."

Sara looked at Lisa. I saw Sara's face had changed from one of sadness to that look she gets right before she springs into action. She crossed the lunch room like a Marine division landing at Guadalcanal.

Sara stood right in front of Lisa and said, "Say you're sorry."

"What...I...how?" was all Lisa was able to get out.

Lisa stared at Sara, an enemy she had created with her own racist words. Shocked by Sara's invasion of her space, she looked away.

"Darn it! Say you're sorry!"

Lisa looked around and realized everybody was watching. She stammered, "I'm...sorry."

"Good," said Sara, "now we can be friends."

Sara retraced her steps back to me, picked up her tray and moved back to Lisa's table and sat down. I, of course, followed.

With tears pouring down like rain, Lisa said, "I didn't want to hurt you. I was just so envious. You had it all together and I was nothing."

"Lisa, you are bright and pretty. You really don't have to be bad to get attention. We're your friends now." She offered Lisa her hand.

Lisa stood up, grabbed the hand in front of her. Somehow, magically, these two former enemies shook hands.

What was next? Maybe something simple, like peace in the Middle East?

"How about I buy you a smoothie after school and then we can go shopping for something for you other than black," Sara said to Lisa. "It's time you got a new wardrobe. If you don't have the money I'll put it on my charge card."

When the shock left her face, I saw a **smile** on Lisa for the first time in weeks.

Chapter Eleven

## Sadie Hawkins

By the middle of May things were just getting back to normal. The legal problems had been taken care of and the bad guys were all behind bars.

I had my best school year ever. Thanks to Miss Gardner, even English class had been fun.

I had always done well in history and science and loved PE. Only math gave me trouble. I would be taking home four A's and one C; not too bad.

The teachers and students seemed to be in cruise-control now that state testing was over. With only two weeks of school left, we were winding down.

Then came the announcement that the Friday before Memorial Day, there would be a Sadie Hawkins's Day Dance. You know the one, where the girls ask the boys. Sharon asked me; remember, the cute girl on the bus. I guess Miss Gardner was right. She did like me and it seemed that she had gotten over the stinky shirt incident.

You might remember that I had kind of a crush on her. So I had to say yes but the whole idea made me nervous. It would be my first date. To make things even more upsetting, I had no idea how to dance.

Sara decided to ask Randy Johnson to go with her but I had a bad feeling about that match. I knew he liked her but he was very religious and I think his church was the kind that believed dancing was a sin. So, I wasn't surprised when he told Sara he couldn't go. She acted unfazed but I could tell she was upset.

But you know; Sara rebounds quickly. She asked Josh Randolph, who said he'd be thrilled to go with her. I was good friends with him so when he agreed, I was jazzed about the whole thing.

I thought the most amazing thing of the whole year were the changes that Lisa Kearney went through. Befriended by Sara and freed from the abuse of her father and brother, she seemed to flourish. The ugly black wardrobe was gone and Sara helped her. Her grades improved. She seemed to blossom like a rose.

Then her mother disappeared. The rumor was she took off for the West Coast with some Hells Angels. Lisa hid at home after school for three days. She figured that if Social Services didn't find out, she could at least finish the school year. But the landlord came looking for rent and she was taken away to a meager group home in East Middletown.

This time it was not Sara's turn to rescue the girl. My parents decided to act; with me feeling somewhat guilty about her father and brother being in prison.

Mom and Dad called Joey and me into their office for a meeting. Mom made a proposal that was a total surprise.

"How would you two feel if we took Lisa Kearney into our family as a foster child?"

My mouth dropped to the floor. I could not have been more shocked than if the Mississippi had turned itself around and flowed north.

Big Bird just shrugged and looked at me. I kinda thought that he was shocked silent. I felt three sets of eyes peering into my brain.

"How could I say no?" is what came out of my mouth.

So just like that, I had a new sister. It sure put my nervousness about the silly Sadie Hawkins Day Dance into perspective. At least Lisa would have her own room. Mom and Dad were giving up their office.

I felt it was my job to find my new sister a date. So I proposed the idea to Tom Gibson, a neighbor who was in my English class. He was also my baseball buddy since I was a little kid. Somewhat reluctant about going to a dance, he told me okay, he would do it for me.

I told Lisa about Tom and the dance. But it being a Sadie Hawkins thing, she would have to ask him herself. She lowered her eyes and said, "No, I can't do that, I can't ask him to go with me."

I knew Sara could talk her into it, but Lisa was now *my* sister. I just grabbed her hand, noticing fingernails bitten down to the nubs.

"You don't think I can go without you, do you? And if I don't go, where would that leave Sharon?"

I led her over to Tom's house and rang the bell which brought him to the door.

"Go ahead," I told her. She asked him to the dance with her voice as soft as a whisper.

Tom said, "Sure, Lisa, I'd be happy to go with you."

She whispered, "Thanks."

Then, with tears running down her face, she fled to her new, uncertain space at our house.

"What was that?" Tom asked me.

"Tom, remember your first Little League at bat; how scared you were? Well, multiply that times ten and you can figure out how frightened she feels. Don't worry; she'll be just fine at the dance."

On my way home, I got Sara on my cell. "I think that Lisa can use your support right about now," I told her.

I'm not sure who was more nervous getting ready for the dance, Lisa or me. Unfortunately, in seventh grade you still have to rely on your parents to take you on a date. That meant we all had to parade for pictures before we could depart from each house. Tom was smart enough to walk over on his own, since my Dad was going to be driving us to Sharon's house.

"You look amazing," I told Sharon. She really did; blond hair falling down her back, a short golden gown held up by tiny straps barely doing their job. I guess it's true when they say that girls mature faster than guys because I felt totally unworthy to accompany the beautiful young lady.

Thanks to Sara, I guess I wasn't a complete dance-floor fool. She taught me two basic dances, one for fast, and one where I got to hold Sharon in my arms.

Miss Garner was one of the chaperones. I walked up to her and told her, "I want you to know, you're the best teacher I ever had." She smiled with those big brown eyes.

"I won't be seeing you at the diner anymore. The District told me yesterday that I'll be teaching here next year. If you're in my class next year, be ready to learn."

Somehow, all of us had a good time, even Lisa. She had Sara to lean on and talk to. She danced often with Tom and even laughed at his lame jokes. I was starting to feel like she was going to be all right.

I took Sharon for a moonlight walk before the dance ended. Knowing that Mom was picking us up, I thought this would be my only chance for a goodnight kiss. With my confidence in high gear from my New Year's Eve experience, I moved in on her ruby-red lips.

Sharon took a step back. "What are you doing?" she asked.

"Um, I was, um, gonna kiss you."

Her nose snapped up in the air, headed for the stars. "My mom says only tramps kiss on the first date."

"Sorry, you looked so pretty, I couldn't help myself." Then, I started to laugh. "Really Sharon, only tramps kiss on the first date? You really think that?"

I continued chuckling. I didn't know if she would cry or slap me but suddenly, she joined me. We just started laughing. She compromised and kissed me on the cheek, leaving a red lipstick mark.

"Boy, I sure hope you don't go to hell for that!" Tears of laughter fell from both our faces as I took her hand and moved back to the dance.

Sara looked at us and said, "What the heck is so funny?"

That only set the two of us back into hysterics.

Finally I said with my hand hiding the lipstick on my cheek, "It's our little secret."

So, that's how my seventh grade story ends, with laughter.

I sure hope you liked it.

PS: I'd like to tell you about my summer vacation…but that's another story….

## Roger Raintree's Summertime Blues

The summer of 2014 was the strangest summer of my life. It didn't start out that way.

I was having a normal summer, playing Babe Ruth League baseball, going on bike rides and in July my family went camping with the Fishers. You know, normal stuff. Even my new sister, Lisa, seemed to be doing okay.

After my interesting and weird year in the seventh grade, it seemed nice to just do regular kid stuff.

Then, the Ferguson thing happened. Boy oh boy, that changed everything.

You might have heard about it on the TV news or by reading a newspaper. But if you're like most of my friends, you don't pay that much attention to the news unless something happens in your town. So, like I said, this was a very strange summer.

On the night of August 9, a man named Michael Brown was killed by a policeman, in Ferguson, Missouri. Michael was 18 years old.

Ferguson is just outside of St. Louis and isn't very far from Middletown. That's where I live. We feel like this whole area is part of our hometown.

The saddest part of this story was that Michael was black and did not have a weapon. Darren Wilson, the policeman who shot him was white.

Now, I learned last year that you don't want to come to any fast judgments about things. In my story I wrote about how the Middletown police really helped me. I also learned last year that the police can make big mistakes.

A bunch of us spent the day after Michael Brown's shooting watching the news on TV. All the stations had it on for hours and hours.

My family talked about Ferguson all through dinner.

My dad said, "There's something fishy about the police officer's story."

Mom made salmon for dinner so we all looked down at the fish on our plates and laughed. I think laughing made us feel better.

I said, "They were saying that the cop felt threatened and fired his gun because he had to, but that doesn't seem right, because Michael Brown didn't have a gun or even a knife."

"It could be that the officer was just paranoid after all the trauma he has seen on the police force." Mom said.

"What does paranoid mean?" I asked.

"It means that he was in the state of being scared all the time; like soldiers with battle fatigue," Mom said.

Lisa said with a bit of anger, "Maybe he was just a racist SOB like my father."

Dad said in a very calm voice, "It's obvious that the police officer made a huge mistake but until all the facts are in, let's give him the benefit of the doubt."

My brother Joey, who is also called Big Bird, said, "A lot of our friends are upset about this. We don't think what's going on in Ferguson is fair. Some of the kids are planning to go over and protest for justice."

"Is Sara one of the friends you're talking about?" Mom asked.

Big Bird and I exchanged a look, I nodded. "You know Sara. If she thinks something is not fair, she wants to take action."

Dad asked, "Are you telling me that you all want to go?"

I said, "Sara thinks we have to go. I agree; especially after we did our Pride Day at school last year."

"What do you think Lisa?" Mom asked.

"I think I'm learnin' from you all, if you ain't helping people, you're part of the problem."

Dad smiled and winked at Lisa. "I can see how important this is to you.

The organizers of the rally tomorrow are committed to nonviolence. I would let you go but I am worried that things might get out of control."

"Ah dad!" Joey whined.

Dad held up his hand. "Hey, I didn't say you guys couldn't go. As a matter of fact, I'm going with you."

I can tell you, I didn't sleep much that night. I wasn't dumb; I knew there were some bad guys that lived in Ferguson. You know, gangbanger types that you hear about in rap music and on TV. It made me a little nervous.

But I knew some nice kids from Ferguson; my baseball team played ball there in July. Their team had white and black guys. They won the game and we all went out for pizza afterwards. It was a fun day.

I found out last night that Ferguson is mostly black but has a lot of white people too.

Some people on TV said that Michael Brown was one of the bad guys. I didn't know if that was true or not. In this case it shouldn't matter. Even if he did bad things, the police should not be shooting at unarmed people.

I woke up real early. I showered, got dressed and went to the front porch just as the sun was coming up. The cool air got warm real fast and I was already starting to sweat; just another hot and sweaty Missouri day, without a cloud in sight.

I heard the screen door open and Lisa sat down next to me.

"You okay?" I asked.

Lisa came to live with us after her father and brother were arrested. Her mother took off somewhere and she was left alone. To make a long story short, my parents stepped in and adopted her.

She looked at me with funny smile, shrugged her shoulders then started to say something and stopped. We were both still a little shy with each other. She was just a year younger than me and will be going into seventh grade. She went from being someone I kinda knew at school to being my sister overnight. It was a bit of a shock for both of us.

I could see her thinking.

"What?" I said and waited.

"Ya know, my Uncle Carl lived in Ferguson when I was little. When the ni. . . blacks moved in, he moved out. My daddy and him just went on and on about it like it was the end of the world. Then Uncle Carl sold the gas station and moved to Mississippi where he said those people still know their place."

Two tears slowly streamed down her face. "I don't want to be like them, it all sounds so evil, don't it."

"Wow Lisa you are so brave. You know you don't have to come with us."

She smiled. "Roger, don't you see, I really have to."

"Well Lisa, I'm proud of you."

The crickets started humming in the background. It's funny cause even when they get loud you mostly don't notice them, but that morning I did. A mosquito started buzzing. I felt it on my neck and slapped.

"Got it."

It left a small bloody spot on my hand. Is that what people in Ferguson felt like?

"We'd better go in," I said to Lisa.


Sara Fisher joined our group as we piled into the SUV. Our families have always been best friends. Sara has a younger black brother; adopted after the Haitian earthquake.

Our car zoomed past the few freeway ramps between Middletown and Ferguson. The picketing yesterday had been peaceful but by night, things turned bad, with rocks being pitched at the police and some people got out of control.

We could still smell some teargas that the police used to break it all up.

We signed up at the NAACP desk. A black man who wore a white shirt and a tie said to a group of about 20 of us, "Welcome friends. My name is Tony Larkins and I will be your group leader. Stay with me at all times unless

you hear the word 'Disperse.' Now please raise your right
hand and repeat these words."

" I promise to be nonviolent during this protest."

We all repeated his words.

"Thank you," he said. "We are going to march up
and down the street for the next two hours. You may take a
button or sign from the table. Does everybody understand?"

"Yes," everyone shouted.


Just about eleven in the morning, all the groups
came together and we started marching. I guess there were
about 1000 people, black and white.

I started to get so nervous I could barely walk. Then
I saw a bunch of troublemakers in front of our group. They
were throwing rocks and cussing at the line of police
wearing helmets on the other side of the street.

I went from being nervous to being a little scared.

The leaders of our march called out with bullhorns:

"Stay together, follow your leaders."

Somehow they marched us right between the police
and the troublemakers. We stopped and I wondered what
would happen next. It seemed, both sides pretended like we
weren't even there. Bottles and stones flew above us

towards the police line and the police came at us with batons. Then teargas exploded. Even though it wasn't right near me, my eyes watered and I started coughing. It was awful. I started running even before I heard the bullhorns, "Disperse! Disperse."

Dad yelled, "Run, follow me. Meet at the car."

People took off in all directions with police chasing them. One cop chased my dad who tripped and fell. The policeman was on top of him with his baton, ready to strike.

Suddenly, just behind me Lisa yelled, "Robert Pickens, I know you."

The policeman stopped and stared and released his grasp on my father.

All of us found ourselves back at the car unhurt.

Dad unlocked the car and said, "Let's go."

As the car entered the freeway, Lisa said, "Well I guess we know at least one of those cops is a racist. Pickens used to hang out with my father's group of rednecks."

No one else said anything. I guess we were all a little bit shocked.

We didn't go back to Ferguson after that mess but we couldn't stop watching it on the news. It's the main thing we talked about for weeks.

I feel much closer to Lisa now. It's like we are a real brother and sister.

I'm hanging out less with Sara; it's going to be strange without her in Middletown Middle School. She's looking forward to being in high school. But we sat together just the other day to talk about what happened and how we felt about that day in Ferguson.

She said, "With all that happened in Ferguson, I think Pride Day is more important than ever. I think every middle school should do it."

I said, "Yeah I think so too. But I've learned an important lesson. There's no such thing as good people and bad people. I guess everything is not all black and white. There are lots of shades of gray."

Sara looked at me with a big smile on her face. "You know Roger, you have potential."

Roger Raintree's Seventh Grade Blues

It took all the way until November 24th for the Grand Jury to make up their minds what to do about the whole mess. To sum it all up they said, that after Officer Wilson stopped Michael Brown for robbery, Michael attacked the officer in his patrol car. Wilson fired ten times in self-defense. The last bullet finally killed Mr. Brown. There would be no trial.

I listened closely to the whole Grand Jury report and really I don't know what to believe. It seems like Michael did a whole bunch of things wrong. But--ten shots at close range, really? Even my Dad who has a lot of respect for the police had a hard time with that.

Anyways, after the report, people went nuts in Ferguson. There were riots and buildings burned and more protests. I'm not going to go near the place for a while.

It's all too bad. I hope someday soon, my community can come together and  life can be better for everyone.

For me, I guess, it's like that rock and roll song I've heard my parents listen to:

> *"There ain't no cure for the*
> *Summertime Blues."*

## Acknowledgements:

The book is dedicated to my son Sam. He taught me many lessons about being a kid.

To my wife, Colleen for her support and love while we deal with the realities of Mr. Parkinson's disease. Nobody said it would be easy.

To my editor, Cathy Carsell, for minding my Ps and Qs, something I hate doing.

To my good friends, (you know who you are) who have given me a great deal of support in good times and bad.

To the Solstice Writers, thank you for all your critiques and help making me become a poet. You have made me a better writer.

**Other books by Nathaniel Robert Winters:**

*Finding Shelter from the Cold*
A Young Adult Novel about wolves; a book for dog lovers of all ages.

*Rumors about my Father and Other Stories*
A Memoir-Novella
This was my first book, written after my father's death.

*The Legend of Heath Angelo*
A Memoir-Novella
I met Heath in 1977 at the Nature Conservancy Preserve he created in Mendocino County.

*The Adventures of the Omaha Kid*
A Novel of sports, romance, and the search for love.

*No Place for a Wallflower* A Memoir-Novella
Iola Hitt's Letters of the Second World War. Iola was a young 93 when I met her and wrote about her involvement in World War II.

### *The Penngrove Ponderosa*
A Novel
Surviving the social and sexual revolution of the 1970's in Northern California.

### *Daydream Distractions*
An Anthology
Poems, short stories, excerpts and notations.

### *Past the Future*
A Science Fiction novel of time-travel's effects on history.

### *Black Knight of Berkeley*
A Murder Mystery with futuristic fantasies.

### *Not Quite Kosher*
A Memoir

Roger Raintree's Seventh Grade Blues

**About the Author:**

Nathaniel Robert "Bob" Winters was born in Brooklyn in 1950 and grew up in suburban Long Island. After serving a tour of duty in the Navy he fell in love with Northern California and made it his home.
He graduated from Sonoma State University and received a Master's in Education from California State University Stanislaus. He enjoyed the opportunity to be a high school history and science teacher for the Turlock School District for 33 years.
For many years an avid skier and tennis player, he also coached baseball and soccer. He currently lives in Saint Helena, a small town in the wine growing region of Napa Valley with his wife and son.
Bob has an affinity for nature and loves to travel. His family has hosted foreign exchange students from France, the Czech Republic and Russia.
He has been diagnosed with Parkinson's disease and still writes almost daily.

Made in the USA
Monee, IL
12 May 2023

33247667R00059